Am I a Turkey?

by Carmen Jewell

DORRANCE
PUBLISHING CO
EST. 1920
PITTSBURGH, PENNSYLVANIA 15238

Dorrance Publishing Co
585 Alpha Drive
Pittsburgh, PA 15238
Visit our website at *www.dorrancebookstore.com*

ISBN: 978-1-6366-1540-0
eISBN: 978-1-6366-1712-1

I am a turkey! There can be no mistake, because, you see, my mother is a turkey!

I was one of five eggs my mother sat on, kept warm, and nurtured for twenty-one days. I hatched first, making me the oldest.

It was hard work getting out of the egg, so after a few hours of rest, I was out and about following my mother wherever she went.

There were also times where I would get so tired trying to keep up with her and her long legs, I would give up and catch a ride on her back.

It was another week before the other four eggs in the nest hatched. I was excited to have other turkeys to play with.

My brothers and sister looked different from me. They were bigger and taller. I was a runt!

However, size never stopped us from playing and being a family!

The place we called home belonged to Mr. Eddie and it was BIG—nine acres.

14

There is a house with large trees, a barn, a garden, a tractor, three dogs, two cats, a rabbit, and open spaces to grow and learn about being a turkey.

Living in the country should be quiet, but not my home. So many sounds: cars on the highway, the train behind the house, the wind blowing through the trees, and birds. So many birds!

The hens clucked,

The ducks quacked,

The geese cackled,

The roosters crowed,

The guineas squawked,

And the turkeys gobbled.

This made up the nine-acre community called home.

I loved living on the farm with all the other birds. I grew; however, I noticed I was not getting bigger or taller like my siblings. Something had to be wrong, but I did not understand what.

Mr. Eddie always kept a small pool of water for the ducks and geese to swim in, then one day I saw my reflection. Imagine my surprise: I looked nothing like a turkey!

I also noticed my voice was not the gobble of a turkey. When I opened my beak, the sound belonged to another bird.

"Oh!" I cried. "This cannot be! I'm not a turkey!"

"Does it really make a difference?" my mother asked.

"I am still your mother, and I have loved you since the moment I laid eyes on you. I will love you forever. You are a member of this family, no matter what breed of bird you are!"

That was all I needed to hear: being accepted and loved by my family. The community took me under their wings and helped me realize that although I am not a turkey, I am a magnificent, proud, happy, and extremely loud ROOSTER!

Cock-A-Doodle-Do!!

CPSIA information can be obtained
at www.ICGtesting.com
Printed in the USA
LVHW071054040222
709847LV00004B/77